The Adventures of
Phoebe Meriweather

Alligator Clips

Meryl Leigh

The Adventures of Phoebe Meriweather: Alligator Clips

This book is written to provide information and motivation to readers. Its purpose is not to render any type of psychological, legal, or professional advice of any kind. The content is the sole opinion and expression of the author, and not necessarily that of the publisher.

Printed in the United States of America.

ISBN   978-1-955363-62-4   (Paperback)
ISBN   978-1-955363-63-1   (Digital)

Pen House books may be ordered through booksellers or by contacting:

Pen House LLC
30 N Gould St. Suite 4752
Sheridan, WY 82801
1 307-683-4249 | info@penhousellc.com
www.penhousellc.com

INTRODUCTION

Faerieland...

A magical place filled with magical creatures full of excitement and wonder...unless, of course, you happen to live there. Then, Faerieland was just another province within the magical community of Utopia Serendipity.

Once upon a time, in this magical land of faeries and sprites, there was a young faerie child born by the name of Phoebe. She was smaller than the other children her age, shorter and more pear-shaped than most. Phoebe Merriweather lived with her parents in number 6 at the end of Chestnut Tree Lane. A lovely two story cottage of yellow and white, which was nestled at the edge of Faerie Belle grove, famous for the single Chestnut tree in the center of the field.

Phoebe loved to sit under the flowering Chestnut tree and dream. She would write make-believe stories in her journals, of traveling with friends and discovering new things and peoples, going on quests for hidden dreams, and solving problems no one else could solve. The tree was surrounded by blooms of zinnia's and marigolds, tiny bluebells and daisies all pushing their way through the dense, purple blooms of the lavender to add their color to the scene. Phoebe would sit under a particularly tall, bright red zinnia with her back against the stem of the flower to write her dream's in her journal.

It would soon be her eighth birthday and all the kids from her class were coming to her party. She was excited - and a bit scared, too, since she sensed that something was going to happen that would change her life forever.

ALLIGATOR CLIPS

Once upon a time, in the magical land of faeries and sprites, there was a young faerie child born by the name of Phoebe. She was smaller than the other children her age, shorter and more pear-shaped than most. But, what made Phoebe such a special little faerie was that she had been born with Stunted Wing Growth Syndrome. SWGS was a very rare disease that occurred in only one out of every 222,000 faeries. It also meant that Phoebe would most likely never be able to fly!

Phoebe's parents were saddened by the news of their child's handicap. They decided that they would not tell anyone in Faerieland of this problem. They wanted their daughter to have a normal faerie life for as long as possible.

They also never told Phoebe.

In the morning on the day before her eighth birthday, Phoebe looked out her bedroom window over the fields of Faerieland and wished she could go outside. It was a beautiful spring day and she had been cooped up in her bedroom for the last three days with a slight case of floppy wing.

Phoebe's bright red hair glinted in the sunshine as she stood on her tiptoes at her bedroom window. She could see butterflies floating in the air over the flower fields and she watched the bees, busy as ever, flit from flower to flower, collecting pollen and nectar for their hives.

"Oh, why do I have to be cooped up inside?" Phoebe thought. "I picked an awful time to be sick. But, I am feeling better. I hope I can still have my birthday party tomorrow." Phoebe wished that to be so. She wished and wished as she stood at the window, thinking that the more she wished the better her chances were of her wish coming true.

Phoebe heard footsteps coming up the stairs. She quickly jumped into bed and pretended to be asleep just as her mother opened her bedroom door. "Good morning my little princess," Mother said as she put down the breakfast tray. "How are you feeling today?" She felt Phoebe's forehead, looked in her eyes then turned back the covers so Phoebe could sit up in bed. Smiling to herself, Mother checked the healing process of Phoebe's wings with a gentle touch.

"Well, I think that a little sunshine will do you a lot of good today." Her mother spoke as she placed the tray on a small table in front of Phoebe. "So, when you are ready just tell me and we will take a little walk outside."

Phoebe was so excited that she jumped off the bed nearly upsetting the tray. "Mom, I'm ready! I'm really ready," she said dancing around her bedroom. "I was just wishing that I could be well so that I can have my birthday party tomorrow. Now, I can!" Phoebe was so happy! Mother laughed and taking Phoebe's hands, danced around the room with her.

"Okay! Get dressed and come downstairs," Mother said. Your Father and I would love to have you join us." Still laughing, she left the room with the same tray she had come in with.

After breakfast Phoebe went for a walk with her parents. Father was trying to show Phoebe how to fly. "It's like this, Phoebe," he said fluttering his faerie wings. You've got to spread your wings out as far as you can so you can catch the air currents. That will help give you lift as you learn how to fly. The breeze will help you to float in the air. Then by turning first this way and then that way you find that you can turn yourself, first left then right, up then down. Do you see?"

Her father demonstrated flying and flitting over and over again as Phoebe tried desperately to copy him. "I just can't seem to fly. I don't think my wings are big enough yet," she said, sadly. "Will they ever grow, do you think?"

"Of course they will, honey," said Mother quickly. "You are simply growing at a slower rate than the other faerie children your age – you're that much smaller. Don't worry, everything will work out just fine. Just give it some time." Then she thought, "In the meantime, it may be, just maybe, that the special exercises Granny taught to me when I was little will help you, too."

Phoebe spent the next several hours outside practicing the exercises her mother had shown her. She practiced and practiced until her wings hurt and she was mentally exhausted. Phoebe wondered "Will I ever be able to fly like the other faeries my age?" She went to bed that night determined that she would practice everyday until she could finally learn to fly.

Sometime after midnight, in the very early morning hours of her eighth birthday, Phoebe was awakened by a loud thumping noise. It was coming from her closet! She sat up in bed just as the door opened and a large white rabbit walked out. The rabbit was wearing a bright yellow vest and a green bow tie with bright blue polka dots. He fiddled with something that seemed to be attached to his vest pocket as he talked to no one in particular – "Oh, bother. I'm late again. I can never get this pocket watch to keep track of time properly. It's always sending me here and there at the wrong time. And, I'm always late! Oh, my goodness…" he said jumping back at the sight of Phoebe sitting up in bed, her round green eyes staring at him in astonishment.

"Well, I suppose you are wondering what I am doing here, right?" Phoebe nodded her head yes, wondering if the rabbit would explain who he was. "Well, yes, of course you are! How silly of me. Well, you see it seems to be your birthday – did you know that? – Oh, of course you did. It is after all *your* birthday and…. The rabbit went on and on about something this and nothing that until Phoebe had had enough.

"Will you please just get to the point!" she impatiently interrupted. "Who are you and why are you standing in my bedroom in the middle of the night?"

"Oh, yes, yes, yes. Terribly sorry, yes, of course, I am Professor Carroll Mouse," he said with a flourish, "and yes I know, it's a very silly name for a rabbit, but there it is. Most everyone calles me Mouse, just Mouse, never Professor Mouse, never Carroll, just Mouse..."

"Yes, but will you just get to the point!"

"Get to the point, get to the point. I must get to the point. After all, if I don't how ever am I going to give you this?" He seemed to puzzle over his thoughts as he pulled something oddly shaped from his pocket, wrapped in pink and yellow polka dot paper with a matching bow.

"What is that?" Phoebe asked, staring at the object in the rabbit's hands. "Is that for me?"

"Why, yes it is, if your name is Phoebe," stated the rabbit. He walked over to the bed and sat down beside Phoebe. "Go ahead," he said, as he handed her the object. "Unwrap your present. Then I'll explain it to you."

Phoebe tore open the small package with excitement. There, nestled in some silky pink fuzz, sat a most unusual watch. It had a clock face with a big hand and a little hand. She had seen those before in school. She was learning how to read time by using a clock. But, what the watch also had were some unusual buttons encircling the outside of the clock face. They had words written on them like *Enter* and *Esc* and *Control* and *Alt* and *Del*. 'What were those for?' she wondered.

Mouse picked up the watch and secured it around Phoebe's wrist. "Now, for a lesson on the proper use of your time machine."

"Time machine?" questioned Phoebe "What do you mean?"

"Yes, yes. Just let me explain. You can ask all the questions you like after I'm finished."

So Mouse proceeded to explain the tiny buttons, what they were for and the do's and don'ts of each – how to activate the time machine and how to move from place to place.

"And, only in cases of dire emergency do you ever hit these three buttons together. When you do, your mission will immediately abort. You'll be thrown back here and locked out. And, then the whole system will go dead."

Phoebe looked curiously at the white rabbit, cocking her head to the right, thinking, 'Mission? What mission?'

"I'm the only one who can fix the problem," Mouse continued. "It's such a bother. Very complicated indeed, and I don't like it one bit when I'm called away from my tea! So, don't do it! Emergency only, emergency only! Keep it safe. Keep it secret. Any questions?"

Any questions? Was he kidding? Of course I have questions, thought Phoebe. But, where to begin… "So, let me see, if I touch this button that says, 'Enter' then I'll start the time machine. If I hit this one that says 'Esc' it will take me back to the first window? I don't understand. What do you mean? What window?"

"Yes, yes. This 'Esc' button will take you back to the first window where you make your choices." Seeing the puzzled look on her face he continued, "You'll see when you get there. Talk with Mother Board. She'll introduce you to Ram and Rommy. They will help guide you through the windows."

"Oh, bother! I've got to go. I've stayed too long, stayed too long. Happy birthday Phoebe," he said. And in a poof of faerie dust he was gone.

Phoebe found it very hard to get back to sleep after the white rabbit had vanished. She tossed and turned and tossed and turned till she was so tired of not sleeping that she actually dozed off. She dreamed of large white rabbits and melting watches, of always running here and there climbing through windows and trying to find that big white rabbit. When she woke up again, Phoebe was exhausted and confused.

She got out of bed and made her way down the stairs to the kitchen to get a glass of water. Her mother and father were sitting at the kitchen table talking when Phoebe walked in.

"My goodness! Look who's here. What got you up so early this morning, Princess?" asked Father. Mother watched as Phoebe sleepily crawled into her father's lap to snuggle.

"I just wanted a glass of water." Phoebe was quiet for a while and drank the glass of water her mother handed to her. Her parents waited. They knew there was something else Phoebe needed to share with them.

She crawled off her father's lap and sat in her chair at the table. "Well," she started, "I didn't sleep very well. I was dreaming about a very large white rabbit and watches that were melting. I was running and crawling through windows trying to catch up with the rabbit, but I don't think I ever did. I'm so tired and confused, I don't know what to think."

"Was this a very tall, very fat white rabbit?" Father asked, winking at Mother.

"Yes! How did you know?

"Oh, he came to me a time or two when I was still a little one. We went on some wild adventures through lands I'd never heard about. He's a clever rabbit, that one. He's Alice's rabbit, did you know?"

Phoebe remembered reading the story of "Alice in Wonderland". Is that all her dream was about, she wondered? "But, I think he gave me something – a present."

"Don't worry yourself about your dream, Princess," said Father. "It's your birthday! And I for one would like to know what my birthday girl wants to do today?" Father smoothed back Phoebe's curly red hair as he talked. Mother set out a wonderful breakfast with all Phoebe's favorites. Phoebe soon forgot all about her dream.

That afternoon Phoebe had the most wonderful time with all her friends at her birthday party. There were lots of balloons and flowers and presents with pretty papers and ribbons that she ripped into with glee. They played games and ate ice cream and cake and talked and laughed for hours. Every boy and girl faerie there could fly, except for Phoebe. But, luckily, no one seemed to notice.

And, then, there was one last gift from her Great Aunt Dahlia of a tiny, pink wristwatch that made Phoebe remember her dream about the white rabbit. There was something about the watch…. "Oh, my!" exclaimed Phoebe. "I remember!" Phoebe raced up the stairs to her bedroom. She remembered that she had put the unusual watch in her special keepsake box in her closet. Phoebe knew it would be safe there.

"Mouse told me to keep this a secret – I can't even tell Mom and Dad." Phoebe was excited. She wanted to try out her new time machine watch right then. "I'd better wait until after the party and Mother and Father think I have gone to bed before I try out the new watch." She put it back in the special box and hid it away.

By eight o'clock, Mother had tucked Phoebe into bed for the night. Phoebe waited listening for Mother's footsteps to fade away down the staircase before she got out of bed. "I'd better get dressed first," Phoebe thought. "I don't want to run off somewhere in my pajama's. I don't know who I'll meet!"

Phoebe bunched up her pillows under the bed covers so it would look like she was in bed. She knew that Mother and Father liked to check in on her to make sure she was really sleeping. Phoebe had been caught several times reading under the covers with her firefly light.

She went to her closet and removed the magic watch from its hiding place. Phoebe fixed the strap to her wrist. She was very nervous. She stood looking at the tiny buttons around the watch face, praying that she wouldn't get lost in some otherworld time warp. Then she pressed the Enter button….

Phoebe was instantly pulled into the world of cyber space, falling through layer upon layer of brightly colored bands of light. Small points of light raced past her in all directions. Suddenly, Phoebe realized she was not falling, but flying! She could fly! As she turned and tumbled this way and that, Phoebe found that she pulled parts of one color band into another. She was painting pictures with the color bands. She found that if she dipped her left shoulder just a little she could turn to the left, the right shoulder and she turned right. If she pulled her wings in tight to her body she could dive bomb like a bird. She felt wonderful and free!

Phoebe was having a terrific time flying through the colors of cyber space. As she looked at her painting she realized that parts of the picture were forming into something else. Something that looked three-dimensional! The space began to look like a landscape of some kind – like someplace outside, but it was inside, too. As she watched, the landscape began to form shapes and funny objects she had never seen before in Faerieland. Phoebe wondered where she was – what magical land had she tumbled into.

Then she saw shapes of colored light coming toward her – walking toward her! Phoebe wondered why they were walking when she could fly? One of the lights came together into the shape of a boy just about her age or a little older. She wasn't exactly sure.

"Hi," he said. "My name is Ramon Arturo Menendez, but you can call me Ram. Follow me. Mother Board is eager to speak with you."

Phoebe followed Ram through a maze of colored pathways. Ram was speaking to her about things she could barely understand – the meanings of the different colors and where each color path would take her. Phoebe was so confused. She did not realize that they had been following the blue line until it stopped in front of a very large blue door. Ram knocked twice then opened the door for Phoebe to enter.

"This is where I leave you for a while, Princess. But, I'm sure we will be seeing a lot of each other, now that you are here. Bye, Phoebe."

Before Phoebe could respond, she heard her name being spoken again. As she turned toward the sound of this new voice she wondered, "How did they know her name?"

"Phoebe, my dear. I'm so glad you came. I'm Mother Board. I'm sure Ram told you about me. Yes? Well, perhaps not. Sometimes I think that if it were not for Rommy that boy would never remember anything.

"Let me be the first to welcome you into *The **S**ociety of **G**adfly **W**innowing **S**pecialists*. We have been anxiously waiting your coming for a very long time now.

"The thing is, we have a few bugs in our system – these gadfly's are really such troublemakers! But, it's a bit of a problem that only you can solve."

"Wait, please. First can you tell me exactly where I am?" asked Phoebe. "I don't understand any of this."

"Please sit down, dear, and I'll explain things as I understand them."

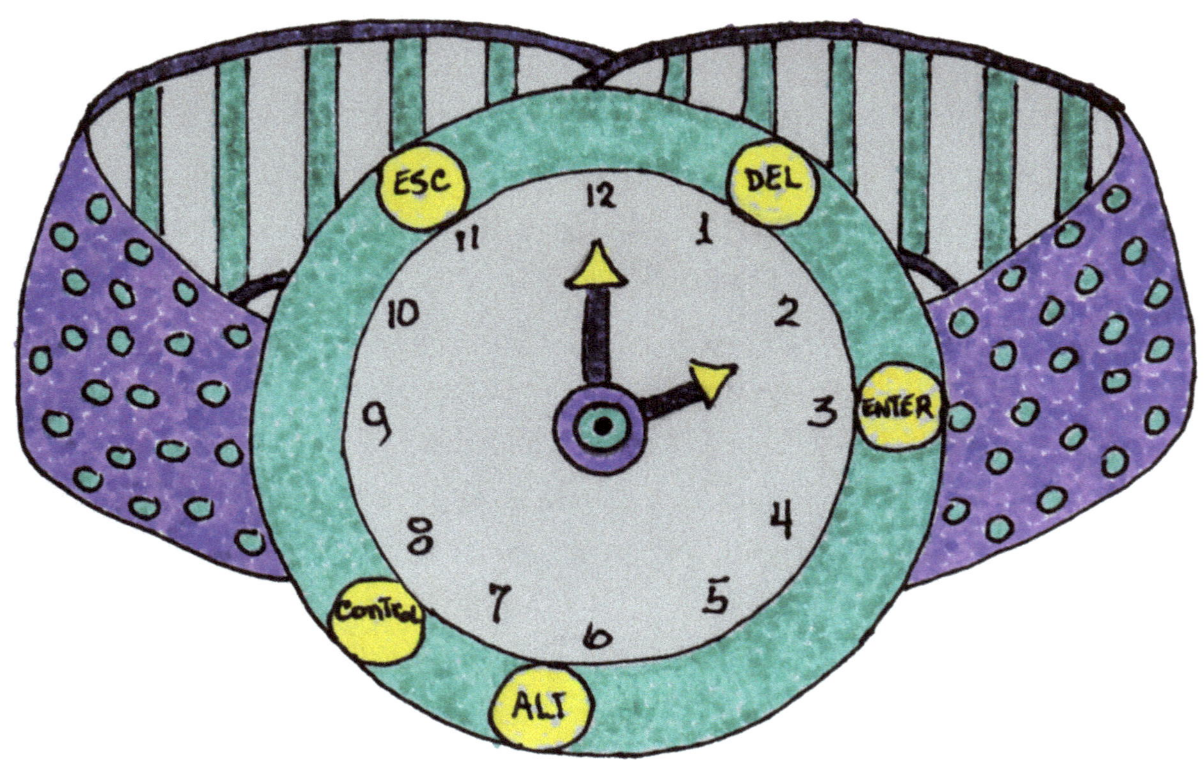

Phoebe sat and listened for what seemed like hours as Mother Board spoke about gadflies and viruses, about cracked windows and gigabyte leakage.

"Well, yes, I think I do see," interrupted Phoebe, "but what does this have to do with me? She had stopped Mother Board in mid-sentence, something no one ever did because it just wasn't polite. But Phoebe was impatient. She watched Mother Board, waiting for a reply.

Then another question popped into Phoebe's head. "And, what makes me so special to you that you had to wait for more than a hundred years for me to be born?"

"Now, that question I can answer with confidence," said Mother Board. "You are the only faerie small enough to fit through the cracked windows. All other faerie's your age are simply too big - their wings can't fold into their bodies close enough. They would get caught on the jagged edges of the cracked windows.

We know this because many, many cycles ago, we asked Faerieland for help. Many tried. Many were injured and disfigured. And, some died trying. Then a young orphan faerie by the name of Earnest said that he would give it a try. We feared for his life. He was only eight years old at the time. And, he was so small that the other faeries made fun of him. But, he desperately wanted to help.

"They told him 'You can't fly. Your wings are way too short.' They questioned how he thought he was going to move around in cyber space if he couldn't fly. They laughed at him and never took him seriously. But, I did.

"I realized that he might be our one and only chance to save our world. He was small enough to get in through the cracked windows without being hurt. I could see that. And, his wings might not get caught like the others. So, I took a chance and allowed Earnest to enter our world.

"He was with us for over a hundred and fifty years! Earnest was a miracle worker! The best Gadfly Winnowing Specialist we had ever had. It was Earnest who began the society. Back when he was still alive, he would recruit other small faerie's to assist him.

"But, they have all retired now and several have passed on. Faerieland has forgotten that we co-exist with them. They've forgotten what wonderful work those small faeries did to keep our world alive. We no longer exist in their memories."

Mother Board looked so sad as she ended her story that Phoebe almost cried.

"We have to start building up the society once again, now that you are with us, Phoebe," she said, looking directly at Phoebe.

"But, I can't do this. I'm only a little faerie girl. I don't even know how to fly!

"Of course you can, Phoebe dear. Your are the perfect faerie for the job, and we have waited so long for your arrival. You are the exact height that Earnest was when he came to us. And your wings are close enough to your body that I just know that you will be able to slip through the cracks safely."

"So, because I'm small and my wings are little, I'm special," questioned Phoebe?

"Yes! That's it exactly. We have discovered that all faeries with extra small wings have exceptional courage."

"Wow! I never thought..." said Phoebe, feeling at a loss for words. She trusted Mother Board and with that trust grew Phoebe's courage to do her very best. She would become as indispensable as Earnest.

"Tell me what I need to do and I'll get started," declared Phoebe.

"Oh, that's wonderful, Phoebe. I like your spirit. I'm sure that we will become very good friends. Right now I think it would be best for you to return to your world and get some sleep. You are going to need your strength for this first assignment. Come back to us after you have had your breakfast. We'll go over your assignment then."

"Okay," said Phoebe, hesitating.

"What is it, dear?" asked Mother Board. "Are you confused as to how to return to your world? Is that it?" Phoebe nodded her head. "Let me show you how easy it is for you, then. It's all on your wristwatch. Just push the 'Esc' button twice and you will instantly return to the exact place you were before you accessed our realm."

With a smile and a nod to Mother Board that she understood, Phoebe pushed the 'Esc' button twice. She instantly found herself transported back to her bedroom, just like Mother Board had said she would.

It was very quiet in the house. Phoebe tiptoed softly to her closet and carefully put her new wristwatch away in its hiding place. Then she changed into her pajamas and crawled into bed. She was excited about her new experience and lay in bed wide-eyed and awake thinking over everything that had happened, wondering what tomorrow would bring. Exhaustion finally took its hold and Phoebe drifted off into a deep and peaceful sleep.

Phoebe awoke refreshed and excited. It was Saturday and she had all weekend to pursue her new adventure into cyber space. She quickly dressed, took her time machine watch from its hiding place and dropped it into her skirt pocket. Then she ran downstairs to have breakfast with Mother and Father.

"And what do have planned to do today, my Princess?" asked Father.

"I thought I'd go to my favorite spot under the chestnut tree in the big flower field," said Phoebe.

"Oh, are you going to practice your flying and flitting? Asked Mother.

"Well, that's one of the things I'm going to do, but I'm not sure what else."

Her parents looked proud as Phoebe left them that morning.

Phoebe zoomed off to her favorite spot under the flowering chestnut tree. Her eye caught sight of a large chestnut that had recently fallen to the ground. It was such an unusual shape that she picked it up and put it into her skirt pocket. 'I'll do something with this later,' she thought.

Once she was safely concealed among the tall flowers at the base of the tree, Phoebe pressed the 'Enter' button for the second time. The color bands of cyber space appeared all around her and she felt weightless once again. She was back!

This time Phoebe knew to follow the blue line to Mother Board's door. She found Ram waiting for her there with a big smile on his face. He knocked twice, as before, on the large door then opened it for Phoebe to enter. This time Ram stayed with her in Mother Board's chambers.

"I'm ready to get to work," she said to Mother Board. "What do I need to do?"

"You and Ram will need to go to our main library to speak with Romesh – we call him Rom or Rommy – he's our head librarian. It is Rom who knows everything about everyone here in cyber space. Without Rom we would truly be lost, for we would be without any memory. Even Ram would eventually forget, and that would be cataclysmic!" Ram nodded his head in agreement.

"So, Ram, I believe the time has come. Please take Phoebe to see Romesh. He will need to inform her of her mission. Also, I want you to assist her in any way you can to get the job done quickly and safely, understood?"

"Yes, Ma'am. Phoebe, if you will please follow me." Ram bowed slightly toward her as he swung his left arm in a wide sweeping arc toward the door. With a courteous 'thank you' to Mother Board, Phoebe followed him out the door.

Phoebe was introduced to Romesh – "Please call me Rommy." – and the cyber space library. It was a huge place with books and tapes and diskettes of all varieties. The library room was so tall that Phoebe couldn't even see the ceiling. And, Ram said the basement had even more floors of information stored there that only Rommy knew how to access. It was really quite impressive.

"Isn't there anyone else to help you, Rommy," asked Phoebe? "I mean, how do you remember where everything is all the time?"

"Now, that is a secret – but I have Ram here to act as my secretary. He keeps me straight and on the right path. Without him, I might wander around and get lost in the stories all around me. I just love books! Don't you?"

"Yes, I do. But, Mother Board has sent me to you because there is something for me to work on. She said that you would tell me all I need to know."

"Oh, yes," said Rommy. What we have is a cracked window – well, there are several windows actually, but you can fix only one window at a time, you see. At any rate, we have a cracked window, as I said, in section "A" of the Alpha quadrant. I can tell you how to get there and what to look for, but I'm afraid that I do not know the actual problem. I also do not know who is having the problem. I only know where it is located. Do you understand my complications, Phoebe?"

"Yes. Can Ram help me?"

"You bet! Ram can collect all the information you will need from the archives. The two of you can go over them and work out a plan. All I can do is direct you in and around the library, here. Ram can move with you through cyber space, but he is not able to go through the cracked windows. Once you go through the window you will be on your own. You will have to solve the problem by yourself."

"Alright. I think can handle that," said Phoebe, and thanked Rommy for his help. She then gave Ram the order to find the information they would need. As soon as Ram rushed off to collect the first of the books, Phoebe sat down at a large table to wait. Within moments Ram had begun to pile books and tapes and diskettes in neat little stacks on the table in front of Phoebe. He moved at lightening speed. Phoebe thought it would be best to wait until Ram was standing in front of her once more before she tried to look at anything. She did not have to wait long.

When he was seated across the table from her, she peered between the stacks of diskettes and tapes and looked into a grinning face. "Wow! That's a lot of information. Where do we start?"

"Book one. How about I walk you through the windows set-up."

So, for the next few hours Ram explained to Phoebe how to enter and exit various windows. They talked about which windows she could layer – stack up like files, one over another – and which windows she could close.

"But, never, never close the very first window you access because that is your only way to get back here. If you close this window then I can't help you – even Rommy won't be able to bring you back. Your only choice will be to abort and exit into your world. The problem with that is that you will have to wait for Mouse to fix your system again before you can come back to us. Do you understand?"

"Yep. I got it! So, are there any tools I can take with me, or won't they pass through the cracked windows?"

"They won't go through," said Rommy, who had been eavesdropping. "Sorry, but you will have to use your own creativity to work out the problem. There is nothing else to be done. Do you have any other questions that either Ram or I can answer for you?"

"No. I guess I know what to do, as much as I can know without trying."

"So, are you ready to get to work, Phoebe," asked Ram?

"You bet! Let's get to it and do it!"

Standing in front of the main window to cyber space, Phoebe was faced with a number of choices. The window had so many folders and symbols that it took Phoebe some time to figure out what each symbol stood for. She was searching for the key that would access the Alpha quadrant. From there she knew that she could search further for the cracked window.

Ram stood by her side, watching and waiting. He could almost see Phoebe's mind working through the problem before her. He could tell that she was a very smart little faerie, and he was proud to be able to work with her.

A-C
D-F
G-J
K-M
N-P
Q-S
T-W
X-Z
CLAC
Complete
Library
Access
Computer

"Found it!," exclaimed Phoebe. "All I do is touch the screen, right?" Ram nodded his head in answer. "You will be able to come with me through each window until I reach the cracked one, yes?"

"Yes, but I may have to stay behind a window or two. It will depend on what we encounter. If you require further information that we have not prepared for, then I will have to stay with the window that can answer those questions. I will be able to stay in contact with you through your watch. Just push the control button when you hear a beep from me, okay?"

"Okay. Well, here goes nothing!"

Phoebe touched one of the symbols on the screen and suddenly she and Ram stood inside a hidden folder. Phoebe searched through the various files looking for the trail of the gadfly. The trail would lead her to the cracked window, she was sure.

"These gadflies are clever little bugs. But, they are messy – finding their trail isn't all that hard. Finding the right one that leads to the cracked window, now *that's* difficult," Phoebe mused. "Ah ha! Let's try this one."

She tugged a file out of a large stack and opened it. Inside were several documents on several different subjects. But, they all had one thing in common – the gadflies had walked over every one and left their footprints, not to mention lots of candy wrappers. They were major litterbugs! Phoebe had to clean out the files before she could find a trail to follow.

"What do these flags mean, Ram?" Phoebe showed him the documents with several yellow and red tabs attached.

"Oh, those are memory alerts. The yellow flags are for caution, meaning be careful when you go to find the bug. The red ones are far more dangerous – don't try those until you've got the knack of finding the gadflies."

"Okay. And what about orange tabs," Phoebe questioned?

"Orange! Oh, my – Rommy will have my head for missing that one!"

And, without so much as a simple 'be right back' Ram was gone. Phoebe was stunned, and stood there a few moments in confused silence. Then, poof! Ram was back.

"Sorry about that. To answer your question, the orange ones are jobs that I have to work on or fix. I got to that one," he said, pointing to the file, "just before Rommy spotted the mistake. Lucky for me you found that one, thanks!"

"No problem. Next time give me some sort of warning before you do that disappearing act, okay?"

"Right!"

"How did you get back, anyway – or rather, how would I get back if that was me?"

"Simple," said Ram. "You press the "Esc" button on your watch and it will bring you right back here." He demonstrated with his own watch, vanishing and popping back with ease. "Just remember to hit the button only once – two times will take you out of this folder and back to the main window in the library - where we are, actually. So, if you should accidentally do that – well, you'll have to remember which symbol you touched to get us here in the first place."

"Okay, understood. Now, what I need to do is to check out the yellow tabs, not the red ones." Ram nodded in confirmation. Phoebe searched through the document's looking for gadfly trails. Finding nothing obvious, she decided that there was only one way to understand how the system worked. She would have to choose a flag and go through.

"Wait for me here, Ram. I'm going to try one." Phoebe pinched the tab between her thumb and first finger and … she was off.

She wound up in a green field where the grass was close cropped. She could see another flag in the distance on top of a tall pole. She wondered where she was. As she looked all around she searched for gadfly trails going through the grass. She began to walk toward the flag. "Say, this is beginning to look like a golf...."

Suddenly something small and white went whizzing past her head. Phoebe hit the "Esc" button on her watch and popped back out of the yellow tab in front of Ram.

"That was a golf game in there!" she declared.

"Whoops! My problem." Ram proceeded to draw diagonal stripes on the yellow tab with an orange marker. "I'll fix that game later. Why don't you try another yellow flag."

Phoebe tried a few more, popping in and out with ease. She had only one more tab to go within this file and she still hadn't found the trail she was looking for. She wondered, 'would it always take this long to find the cracked window or would it get easier with practice?'

Ram seemed to read her mind. "You know, next time it probably won't take so long to go through all these files and windows. You will probably think of shortcuts that we can use, ones that I haven't come up with before – that will make things a lot easier, not to mention a lot faster. So, just hang in there."

"Thanks! I didn't think of that. But, I have a question, Ram. How do I communicate with you once I'm inside a file or another window?"

"Oh, just push your "Control" button and it will beep me. I can beep you the same way. See?" He pushed his control button and Phoebe's watch began to sing, 'Somewhere Over the Rainbow'. She laughed with delight.

"That's great! So, I don't need to pop back out just to ask a question. Only if it's the wrong window or document, right?"

"Right! But, remember, when you find the cracked window, you and I can no longer communicate once you pass through the cracks."

Nodding her head in understanding, Phoebe looked at the last yellow flag on the last document in the file. "This document seems to be talking about the water quality in the northwest section of Quadrangle 2. Where do you suppose Quadrangle 2 is located?"

Ram looked the document over then said, "Looks like Quadrangle 2 is within the boundaries of Faerieland. Wait here a minute while I ask Rommy to locate it for us."

When Ram returned he informed Phoebe that Quadrangle 2 was their name for the area around Allentown in Faerieland. "Rommy believes that the gadflies have somehow managed to break through the confines of cyber space and affect the physical world of Faerieland," said Ram. "That's going to be quite a problem to fix!"

With a sigh she said, "Okay, I might as well get this last one over with. I'll beep you if I need you." Pinching the tab with thumb and forefinger, Phoebe disappeared.

Ram waited. "She must have found something," he thought. "She's been gone much longer this time." He waited and he waited until he couldn't stand it anymore. He was sure that something had happened to Phoebe – his mind was running wild, making up all sorts of stories about the dangers that she had surely encountered. Ram was kicking himself for having let her go alone.

Suddenly, Phoebe beeped him.

"What took so long," Ram demanded, his voice sounding more irritated than he had intended. "I was getting worried," he said, on a softer note.

Phoebe did not answer his question. Instead she said, "I need you here with me. I think I have found the gadfly trail."

He appeared at the edge of a mangrove swamp. There was a small stream flowing out of the swamp to the left. Phoebe walked to the stream and carefully walked down the bank to the water's edge. Ram followed.

"I've been through two more windows following this trail." She pointed at some markings that followed a zigzag pattern. Ram could see a faint trail of footprints embedded within the marks on the damp ground. But, the tip-off that this was a fairly fresh trail was the discarded candy wrappers among the debris.

"I'm going to guess that you followed the candy wrappers, right?" Phoebe nodded with a big grin on her face.

"Yep! And, I found fresh footprints, too," she said. "But I had to go through two more windows before I was really sure. Come on. The main window is this way."

Ram followed Phoebe away from the stream and up a short hill. At the top of the rise they could see a small glen of trees just off to the right. The stream wound its way into the trees and disappeared. "We need to go over there," said Phoebe, pointing at the line of trees. "Not inside the trees but just to the outside edge, on the left. This is what took me so long before. It's a long way off – farther than it looks from here."

"You mean you walked," Ram gasped in astonishment. Why didn't you fly over?"

"Fly?" Phoebe had not thought about trying to fly until now. "Well, I never thought…but I guess it won't hurt to try." She was a bit bashful about trying with Ram watching. But, she screwed up her courage and gave it her best effort. Spreading her wings as far as they would go, she fluttered them the way her father had shown her.

A sudden air current caught Phoebe's wings and lifted her off the ground. With delight and determination she flitted her way toward the stand of trees, winding her way this way and that as she adjusted to flying. She was at the edge of the glen in a matter of seconds and had to grab a passing branch to stop her flight. She tumbled to the ground in a jumble of arms and legs.

Ram was at her side in an instant. "Are you alright?"

"I flew! I flew," she cried, thrilled with the new experience. Phoebe was so happy that she danced in circles around the tree where she had fallen. Ram, giggling with amusement, joined in her dance.

"We had better get moving," said Ram, returning his attention to their job at hand. "Where do we go from here?"

Phoebe lead the way around the stand of trees till she came to a dirt path. It was partially hidden by the twisted bramble of a wild raspberry bush. She gathered a few of the luscious ripe berries then carefully pulled back the branches enough to allow passage into the heart of the glen. Ram followed, wondering how Phoebe had found the hidden path.

In the very center of the glen was a clearing. Inside the clearing stood a tall, blue window rimmed in gold. And, at its base were piles upon piles of discarded candy wrappers. The gadflies had been using this hidden window for a very long time.

"So this is where they have been hiding out," exclaimed Ram. "No wonder I have had such a hard time tracking them. I never knew this window existed. Phoebe, you are amazing!"

"Thanks." Phoebe was filled with a new sense of pride and she let it show. She stood a little straighter, walked a little taller and held her head up high. She walked the clearing showing Ram the clues she discovered that told her which window to go through next. Ram agreed with her deductions, admiring her logical, yet creative, mind.

Standing once again in front of the big blue window, Ram watched as Phoebe flew up to the top right corner of the screen just above a small dragonfly symbol.

"Wait!" cried Ram. "We need to tag this window before we go through. That way we will remember to come back and shut it down. We have to stop the gadflies from using this portal."

"Oh! We can do that?" Phoebe flitted back down to land clumsily at Ram's side. "And just how do we do that?"

"Right now," said Ram, "I'll just put an orange flag on the top of the window. I'll be able to see it from our home screen when we return. I can fix the problem then. For now we need it to remain open. It is our link back through." Ram scrambled up the side of the window, planted the orange flag and was back at Phoebe's side before she could speak.

"How do you do that?" Phoebe was awed by his lightning speed.

"I operate on cyber time, Phoebe. You are a bit slower because you are still operating on physical, Faerieland time. You'll move faster as you become accustomed to the search routine, you'll see."

Phoebe hoped that was true, but she wasn't going to hold her breath. She had learned to be patient with herself. She knew that there were some things that just took her a little longer to master. But, master them she would!

With a touch to the dragonfly symbol, Phoebe and Ram were whisked away into the world of insects. The entrance to this world was through what looked like a huge prism but was actually a crystal eye. It was only by following the trail of candy wrappers that they were able to make their way out of the eye and onto the waxy leaves of a lily pad. They now stood in the middle of a large lily pond, thick with gnats.

"Ugh," said Ram, waving his hand in front of his face. "Where the heck are we?"

"This is as far as I've come. I lost the trail and I don't know where we go from here. I was hoping you could figure that out." Phoebe flitted in a zigzag toward the pond's shore and landed a bit unsteadily, but this time she stayed on her feet. "Hey! I'm getting the hang of this. Did you see? I landed on my feet," she said proudly.

Ram zoomed to Phoebe's side. "Let's get out of here and away from these gnats. There's got to be a trail around here, somewhere."

They walked up the grassy slope to the edge of a well-tended flowerbed. Phoebe looked back at the pond. She looked all around the landscape trying to remember why this pond suddenly looked familiar to her. She was sure that she had been here before, on an outing with her parents, perhaps? Shaking her head to clear her thoughts, she looked back at the flowerbed. Ram was watching her.

"This looks really familiar to me, Ram. I'm sure that I've been here before."

"That's not possible. I can't cross into the physical world so I'm fairly sure we are still in cyber space."

Phoebe could see his point. So, where had she seen this pond before? "Oh, I know now! It's the story of the ugly duckling – that's why this pond seems so familiar. I wonder where the ducks are this time of day? Say, Ram, do you think we will get to see the little swan?"

Ram had no idea what she was talking about, so he quickly covered up by shrugging his shoulders and shaking his head a bit as if to say 'I don't know.'

"Don't you just love the sounds of spring? I love listening to the humming of the bees," said Phoebe. "Doesn't it sound wonderful?"

The air was filled with the humming of insects and bees flitting through the flowers. They could hear the gentle wing rustles of the tiny iridescent damselflies hovering over the lily pond. It was quite a while before the rising level of the noise caught their attention. It began as a low din. It grew louder so gradually that at first they did not recognize the danger.

Ram looked up suddenly from his study of the ground. "Listen." He said, touching Phoebe's shoulder. They listened intently for a few seconds. Then, recognizing the danger, Ram stated, "I think we might have a problem. We'd better get under cover right now!"

Shoving Phoebe ahead of himself, they dove for cover just as a squadron of the largest dragonflies Phoebe had ever seen flew over the tops of the flowers, heading for the lily pond.

"Th...th...those dragonflies are bigger than I am!" cried Phoebe, suddenly frightened.

"Hush!" Ram hurriedly put a hand over Phoebe's mouth. "We can't let them hear us. They will eat us alive!"

Phoebe looked up as a second group of giant dragonflies flew over their hiding spot. They watched and listened intently to the communication between the smaller damselflies and the larger, bomber-like dragonflies. Apparently, there had been a report of an invasion in the area. Neither Phoebe nor Ram had seen any sign of an invasion. They wondered what the dragonflies were talking about.

"Sergeant Major, report!" Ram and Phoebe heard the order loud and clear.

"No sign of them yet, sir. The scouts are covering the area around the pond right now. We should have a report shortly," came the reply.

"Widen the search, Sergeant Major. I want those gadflies found and their passageway sealed up before nightfall. Understood?"

"Yes, Sir! General, Sir!"

Phoebe and Ram looked at one another. "Gadflies?" they said, together. The dragonflies were searching for gadflies, too?

"Do you think they can help us?" whispered Phoebe. Ram shrugged his shoulders. He did not know what to do.

"I'm out of my world of knowledge here. Unless you have any bright ideas, I think we had better stay under cover until they are gone."

Phoebe thought for a moment. "No," said Phoebe, having made a decision, "we can't wait that long. I've got to get back home before dinner."

"Oh, don't worry about that. Cyber time is much faster than physical time, Phoebe."

"Really?" she said in wonder. "Still, I don't want to waste valuable time sitting here when we could be finding the cracked window. No, I really think we are going to have to ask the dragonflies for help." She eyed Ram, looking directly at him with raised eyebrows, as though saying, 'well, get on with it!'

"Oh, I get it. You mean that *I* should be the one to ask the dragonflies for help! Great. Just great!" Ram crossed his arms over his chest, huffing and muttering to himself while walking up and back, up and back.

Phoebe waited and watched while Ram had his little temper tantrum. He eventually calmed down and walked back to Phoebe's side.

"Okay," he said quietly, hanging his head. "I'll do it."

Before Phoebe could respond, they heard the buzzing of wings overhead and the radio report of the lead damselfly.

"I've got them, Sir! They're over here, Sir." Pointing a wicked looking tail at Phoebe and Ram he ordered them to stay put.

Ram started to speak, "Look, man, we are not …."

"Don't move or I'll shoot!"

Ram put himself in front of Phoebe and they waited for the squadron leader to arrive. It wasn't long before the air was filled with dragonflies. The flowers and bushes overhead swayed in the breeze caused by thousands of wings in motion. Phoebe held on tightly to Ram to keep from being lifted off the ground.

"How did you get through our radar?" a booming voice demanded.

"We came through the window – you know, the one with the dragonfly symbol…" Ram's voice trailed off as the squadron leader flew in for a closer look. His many faceted eyes took in everything around him, all 360 degrees! He saw Phoebe, paying particular interest to her small wings. He was about to push Ram aside to get to her when Ram stood tall and hugged Phoebe protectively.

"Tell my why I shouldn't just string you up right now and let my troops have you for lunch? I know they are itching to get their hands on you. Especially that plump morsel with the tiny wings!"

"We are not gadflies, Sir," Ram yelled at the leader. "We have been sent here under orders from Mother Board to find the cracked window in this quadrant."

The leader backed away a few feet then touched down and walked toward them. "Mother Board, eh? Well, if that is true," he said to Ram, "then explain that." He pointed at Phoebe.

"Umm," said Ram, clearing his throat. "This is our new Gadfly Winnowing Specialist." Dragging Phoebe out from behind he said, "Phoebe, say hello to the nice dragonfly. That's a girl. Don't be afraid."

"H...hello," she said hesitantly. "I'm Phoebe of Faerieland and we are following the trail of the gadflies in hopes of finding the cracked window. I've been sent to fix it and stop the gadflies from coming back this way."

"Right! Can you help us?" Ram blurted the question out before Phoebe even had time to think. She was stunned into silence.

The squadron leader stood before them, quietly thinking over the problem these two intruders presented. "Well, since you two appear to be searching for the same troublemakers we are," he said, coming to a decision, "we will assist you, but only to the edge of the woods. In turn, you will tell me where you landed when you came through the window."

"Oh, that's easy. We came through over the lily pond, just over there." said Phoebe pointing. "Come on. I'll show you." Phoebe walked off toward the pond expecting the dragonfly to follow.

Of course, he did!

<hr>

"Thank you, Ram," said Phoebe, later. "Thank you for protecting me from the dragonflies. Lucky they turned out to be so nice, though, huh?"

They had ridden on the backs of two of the large dragonflies in the bomber squadron, with the General leading the way across the vast grasslands and flowering fields of their realm. Phoebe and Ram had been dropped off at the edge of a wooded glen where the dragonflies refused to go. "You're on your own from here," the General had said. "Good luck!" And off they flew, back toward the lily pond.

Ram and Phoebe walked into the woods in search of the gadfly trail. Phoebe hoped that they would find another window soon. She was ready to leave the world of the dragonflies. Yet, she wondered why they refused to fly into the forest.

"Keep your eyes out for anything unusual, Ram. There's got to be a reason why the General would not fly into this forest."

"I was just thinking the same thing. It is pretty creepy in here. You stay close, okay? I don't want to lose you in here."

Phoebe smiled to herself. She knew that Ram was as frightened as she was, but he would never show it. She kept an eye out for where she was going just the same. She, too, did not want to lose Ram. She wasn't yet sure enough of her own skills to go on alone. Phoebe was very glad to have his company on this hunt.

They carefully walked the forest trail, watching for anything unexpected, searching for signs of the gadflies. Phoebe and Ram took turns watching the trees while the other searched the forest floor. But, they found nothing – nothing of the gadflies and nothing out of the ordinary.

They were halfway through the forest when they found the clearing. But, there still was no sign of the gadflies – no footprints in the soft soil, and no trail of candy wrappers. The clearing appeared to be deserted. Phoebe sat down on a fallen tree to rest. Ram walked around the outer edge of the clearing.

"There's got to be a trail of some kind around here," he said, walking back to sit next to Phoebe on the tree. "Maybe we need to look at this from a different angle."

"I don't think we did anything wrong, but I agree that we might be looking in the *wrong place*. Tell me, Ram, can gadflies fly?"

"Sure they….Of course! That's it!" Ram stood up suddenly, all excited. "We have been looking in the wrong places. How silly of me not to think of this earlier!"

"What is it? What are you talking about, Ram?"

"Gadflies not only fly, they can become almost invisible! The only way to detect them when they are invisible is to look at the empty space – you know, the space between the leaves of the trees and the trees and the sky. Like that."

"We will be able to spot them that way? I don't understand, Ram. Show me what you mean."

Ram looked up into the trees around the clearing, searching for a glitch in the spaces. He thought he saw one, but just to be sure he looked away for a moment then back at the area where he saw the glitch. It was still there.

"I've found one, Phoebe," he said pointing to the trees overhead. "Come over here, stand in front of me." Phoebe stood with her back to Ram, his right arm stretched out over her shoulder pointing at the spot in the trees. "Follow the line of my finger. Bend your head over, there, can you see it?"

Phoebe trained her eyes along the line of Ram's finger to the empty space above. She was about to give up trying when she caught the slight shimmer of what looked like a candy wrapper caught in between the leaves of the tree.

"I see it! I see it, Ram! It's a candy wrapper!"

"Yep!"

"But, what is making it stay in one place?" asked Phoebe. "Why doesn't it fall to the ground?"

"I'm not sure. There's got to be a reason. Let's see if we can spot why."

Phoebe and Ram stood in place looking at the shimmering spot in the trees. The candy wrapper moved with the breeze through the leaves, yet it did not change its position. A sunray found its way through the thick canopy for a brief moment, but it was enough to light up the rest of the area around the candy wrapper. Then they saw it!

"A spider's web!" they said together.

"So that's why the dragonflies would not fly into this forest. They don't want to get caught in the spider's web!" said Phoebe. "But it seems such a small web to be frightened about."

"Well, that can't be the only web in the forest. Still, if they are all this small I don't see what there is to be frightened about. Anyway, we need to search the trees a lot more carefully from now on."

Phoebe agreed. Together they walked around the clearing searching the trees from their roots all the way up to their tippy tops. They found a small trail but it did not seem to lead anywhere except back to the first candy wrapper. They were walking around in circles.

"I think we need to back track a bit, see if we can find another trail," said Ram.

"Or, perhaps we need to move forward. Either way, we can't keep going around in circles like this. I vote that we move on ahead – how about going in that direction?" Phoebe pointed off to the right of the clearing where she could see another small footpath through the forest. Ram grunted and nodded his head in agreement. Phoebe spread out her wings and took flight, heading across the clearing toward the footpath.

"Wait!" Ram suddenly reached out and grabbed Phoebe's foot, stopping her in mid flight. She came tumbling down in a jumble of skirts making a soft thump on the ground at Ram's feet.

Phoebe was too stunned to speak.

"Sorry, but...."

"Sorry? But, why ...?" Phoebe was so confused. She shook her head to clear out the muddle in her mind.

"Look!" Ram pointed at the center of the clearing.

"Look at what, Ram? I don't see anything."

"We looked all around this place, right? We even walked around the outside edge of this clearing. But, we never looked closely at the center of the clearing."

"Okay. So, what's your point."

"Look carefully, Phoebe," said Ram. He pulled Phoebe in front of himself and pointed toward the clearing's center. "Do you see the spider's web?"

"Oh my gosh! That the biggest spider's web I've ever seen!"

"The question is, what's holding it up?" asked Ram. "It doesn't appear to be attached to anything – there aren't any web lines that touch the ground and there aren't any that attach to the trees above. In fact, it looks like it is hanging in mid-air."

Phoebe could see Ram's dilemma for she, too, couldn't see any anchor lines. Then she had a brilliant thought. "Ram," she said thoughtfully, "remember how we found the last window? Remember where it was located?"

"Yeah," he said slowly. He looked confused, wondering where her line of thinking was headed.

"Remember how all the windows we've found so far have all been in a clearing somewhere?" Ram looked stunned as Phoebe went on, "I'm willing to bet that the spider's web is covering up the window to this world, making it invisible. And," she continued, "I'll bet it is the window that is holding the web in place."

"How do you do that?" Ram questioned in admiration. Phoebe looked at him oddly, not understanding. "I mean, how did you figure this out so brilliantly? You're amazing, Phoebe!"

Smiling bashfully, she said thanks then turned her attention back to the web-covered window. How were they going uncover the window so they could go through? Did they need to destroy the web or was there another way? Could they crawl under, she wondered?

Now that he saw the web clearly, Ram walked around the area, careful not to get too close. He was wondering how they were going to manage this task when he realized that he was being carefully watched. He looked over at Phoebe, but she seemed to be looking at the web and not at him. Ram slowly looked up and what he saw there made him take several clumsy steps back. He landed on his bottom with a thump loud enough to draw Phoebe's attention away from her own thoughts.

"Ram! Are you all right?" Phoebe raced around the clearing to his side. He continued to stare wide-eyed at the center of the web. Phoebe followed his gaze and with a sudden gasp, sat down beside him, dumbfounded. She recovered after a moment and clearly expressed Ram's thoughts perfectly when she said, "That's the biggest, ugliest, most giant spider I have ever seen!"

Now that the spider knew she had been seen, she materialized in the center of her still invisible web, looking very menacing. Appearing to hang in mid-air, she looked to Ram and Phoebe to be several feet in diameter. Their survival instincts had them both scooting back several feet on their bottoms to get out of harm's way.

"What tasty morsels you two will make," she hissed. "I will wrap you up and marinate you until you are so tender your meat will fall easily off your bones. Oh, but you will make a lovely treat. Yes, a very lovely treat indeed." Her words oozed from her as she slowly descended from her web towards the ground.

Ram and Phoebe quickly scrambled to their feet. There was no way they were going to end up as spider food! They ran for the cover of the trees.

"Yes," she hissed out. "Yes, run into the forest. My children will catch you quickly and we shall feast tonight!"

That did it! Something tripped Phoebe's memory of an experience she had had on the flying course at Faerieland Grammar School. "Now, wait here just a minute," said Phoebe, stepping back into the clearing.

"Phoebe, don't…" cried Ram in alarm.

"How can you feast on us tonight if you plan on marinating us until we're tender? Won't that take a while?" Phoebe continued, all in a rage, "You're just trying to scare us. You're nothing but a big bully! And, we don't put up with bullies in Faerieland." Phoebe was alive with anger and she didn't care how big the spider was she was going to scare it right back.

Then she did something that neither she or Ram thought she could. She flew at that spider so fast and with such power that the spider had no time to react. Phoebe slapped that spider right across the face! Then, darting quickly out of reach, Phoebe proceeded to give the spider a lecture on the proper behavior one should accord guests in her realm.

It was such a fiery lecture that the force of it stunned the spider. She had never been challenged before. She, the largest spider in the forest, had never encountered anyone or anything that was not frightened of her size. She scampered back up her web lines to the safety of the center of her web.

"Please don't hurt me," cried the spider, cowering away from Phoebe in fear. "I was only trying to scare you away. That's my job, you see."

Caught off guard by the spider's reaction, Phoebe stopped her tirade. She realized that she had backed the spider into her safety corner and that she, Phoebe, was no longer afraid. She also was no longer angry at the spider. Instead, Phoebe found a growing sense of compassion for her.

"I'm sorry that I frightened you, but you need not have been so rude to us." Phoebe spoke gently to the spider, unconsciously floating in mid-air by the lightning flutter of her small wings. "My name is Phoebe and that boy down there," she pointed, "is Ram. We are here on a special mission from Mother Board following a gadfly trail. We mean you no harm.

"Oh," the spider gasped, "You know Mother Board?"

"Yes. Please, tell me, what is your name?"

"Um, I…I'm the Widow Marguerite." The spider said softly, with hesitation. "How, um, how can I be of service to you?"

"We need to access the window that I believe your web is concealing." Phoebe stopped her train of thought, suddenly recalling something the spider had said. "Did you say that it was your job to scare people away?" she questioned.

"Well, yes, sort of. It's my job to protect this window."

"Is there a way we can access the window without damaging your beautiful web?" Phoebe's compliment hit the mark. Widow Marguerite glowed with pride, rewarding Phoebe with a bashful smile.

"Why, yes, there is," said Widow Marguerite, "but tell me how you came to the knowledge of the window's existence behind my concealing web? What gave it away?"

"Actually, there is nothing out of place that would normally lead me, or anyone for that matter, to believe that there was anything at all inside this clearing. It's only that I've noticed that all of the previous windows we've been through have been in the middle of a clearing. It made perfect sense that this one would be the same. Especially when Ram suggested that we begin to look at the space between the leaves and the trees. That's when we began to see the almost invisible side of things here in your forest. That's how we were able to finally see you."

Widow Marguerite had been descending from her web as Phoebe spoke. Phoebe, naturally, had kept pace, hovering ever lower until her feet finally touched the ground. Ram rushed to her side the instant her feet touched and pulled her back several feet away from the spider. He did not trust the Widow Marguerite!

The sudden force with which Ram pulled her away from the spider shocked Phoebe. She stared at him frozen in disbelief. The Widow Marguerite froze in her tracks.

Quickly coming to her senses, Phoebe pushed Ram away, "What did you do that for? What's the matter with you?"

"Well, excuuusse me!" said Ram, dragging out the word for emphasis. "Pardon me for trying to save your life, your Highness!" Ram was hurt by Phoebe's words. He reacted by getting angry.

"I'm sorry, Ram. I did not mean to say such awful things to you," Phoebe said, soothingly. "It's just that sometimes when I get frightened my temper comes out. I don't mean to hurt you, I just haven't learned to control it yet. Forgive me?"

"Well...okay. But you scare me sometimes, too. You're my responsibility while you are here. Mother Board would *kill* me if I let anything happen to you, Phoebe. We need you here, in cyber space."

"I'm sorry. I understand. I'll try not to get so upset in the future, okay?"

Phoebe heard a shifting noise behind her and turned to see Widow Marguerite only inches away, looming over her head. She gasped at the spider's closeness. Widow Marguerite pulled her head up, stretching back away from her examination of Phoebe's wings.

"I'm sorry," said the spider, 'I was only looking at your wings. They have such a beautiful design that I was trying to figure out how I could copy the pattern. That's all."

Phoebe's heart rate slowed back down. "Thank you for the compliment, Widow Marguerite. I'm flattered that you want to design a web in the same pattern as my wings. Truly, I am. But, what Ram and I need to do as quickly as possible is to access that window. Will you show us how?"

"Of course. Right this way." The spider turned around and walked behind her invisible web. Ram and Phoebe followed. "There," said Widow Marguerite, "you can crawl through my web right here at this design point. See how I have woven in the pattern of a small...."

"It's the letter A!" cried Phoebe and Ram in utter astonishment.

"Yes! Rather genius of me, don't you think? You can get through safely by going between the two legs of the letter." Widow Marguerite pointed out the area to Phoebe. "I did have to fix it recently, just to let you know. Caught one of the gadflies myself, but not before two others made it through."

"Got it. Thanks!" Phoebe carefully made her way through the web, but before Ram could follow her she poked her head back out. "Ram, it's the cracked window. You'll have to stay here while I go on."

"Oh, no way! I'm not staying here without you. I'm going back one window where I know I'll be safe. I'll wait for you there." And, with the touch of a button on his wristwatch, Ram disappeared.

"Well, I never...." stammered Widow Marguerite.

"Well! I suppose that's that!" said Phoebe. "Thanks, Widow Marguerite. I am not sure if I'll be back through this window. I'll have to fix it from the other side. But, I'm sure we will meet again. I'm glad to have made friends with you." Phoebe waved to the spider then disappeared once more inside the web.

Phoebe found an area in the largest crack of the window wide enough for her to safely slip through. She was hesitant to spread her wings, so she climbed carefully down the other side, dropping into the squishy mud below. 'Oh, that's just great,' she thought. 'I've landed in another swamp. Just my luck.'

Sagebrush and creeping vines surrounded the window, hiding it from view. She squished her way through the mud to where she thought she saw an opening in the underbrush. 'At least it's dry here,' Phoebe thought. Getting down on her hands and knees, Phoebe crept through the foliage toward the light ahead. She came out in a place she least expected. She was standing at the edge of a large avocado grove!

Phoebe sensed that something was different in this realm. There were smells here that she had not sensed in cyber space. And, the colors were not as vibrant in this world as they were before. Had she crossed back into the physical world when she crawled through the cracked window?

Phoebe remembered Rommy saying that the gadflies had broken through from cyber space. She also remembered that Ram had told her that once she crossed through the cracked window their communication link would be broken. Phoebe tried to raise Ram on her wristwatch, pressing the 'Control' button like he had shown her. There was no response. That confirmed it for her. She was in the physical world again, and now she was on her own.

Phoebe realized that she would have to be careful not to be seen by any other faeries. Because, she did not know how she would ever be able to explain being in Allentown to her parents, for she was sure that was where she was, now. She must find the gadfly trail, correct the problem as best she could, fix the cracked window and get back to Ram as fast as possible.

Spreading out her wings, Phoebe attempted to fly across the grove. But, as hard as she tried she could not get her small wings to lift her off the ground. Then, a sudden gust of wind caught Phoebe by surprise, lifting her in the air for a brief moment. She felt the excitement of being airborne again. As the wind died out, Phoebe tried to stay aloft as long as she could, flitting this way then that, making a zigzag path back down to the ground.

Phoebe danced with joy. She had flown for the first time in the physical world. She had actually flown! The fact that her flight had been short did not matter. All that mattered was that she had taken her first step toward really learning to fly. She couldn't wait to show her parents. They were going to be so proud of her!

Excited as she was, Phoebe practically skipped through the avocado grove. She wasn't paying particular attention to where she was going, lost in all her excitement. So, when she stumbled upon a young alligator sitting under one of the trees, Phoebe was quite shocked. "Oh my," she gasped, stopping dead in her tracks. She darted behind the closest tree.

Luckily for her, the alligator had not heard her coming so Phoebe had a few moments to observe him. Peeking around the tree trunk, Phoebe noticed that he looked a little sad. He was an unusual shade of light blue-green, rather pretty, actually. Sort of aqua in color. He was wearing an apricot tank shirt with a pair of green shorts the color of young avocados. 'How funny,' she thought. 'Every color he is wearing starts with the letter 'A', except for his tennis shoes, they look rather black, probably cause they're old.

He was tossing an avocado back and forth between his beefy hands. It looked like he had been sitting there for quite some time, she thought. There were several empty avocado shells by his side along with a sharp knife and a spoon. He clearly had been eating the avocados. 'He doesn't look like he would hurt me,' she thought. So, Phoebe took a chance and stepped out into the alligator's view.

He was surprised by her appearance and quickly wiped his face with his hands. He had been told about faeries before but this was the first time he had ever seen one. He thought she looked rather small, though, so he really wasn't sure he guessed correctly. "Hi there. Where did you come from?" he asked.

"Uh, back there," she stammered, vaguely indicating a direction somewhere behind her. "Who are you?"

"I'm Albert," he said, "Who are you?"

"You're an alligator," Phoebe said almost to herself.

"That I am," he said proudly. "And you are...?"

"Oh, sorry. I'm Phoebe." Quite automatically, she extended her hand for a welcome handshake. There was a moment of awkwardness between them.

Albert stood up then, dusted himself off and extended his own large hand in greeting back to Phoebe. Her hand was very small in his as they shook hands. And, he was so tall! Phoebe had to tip her head way back to look up at Albert.

"Are you a real faerie?" Albert asked in awe.

"Why, yes I am. Have you never seen a faerie before?"

No, he hadn't. Albert suggested that they sit on the ground under the avocado tree and talk. Phoebe sat cross-legged and they talked for quite sometime, getting to know each other. It seemed that they had something in common. They both had a secret fear that kept them form doing the normal things faeries and alligators did at their age. For Albert it meant he got teased a lot.

"Well, that just doesn't seem right, Albert. We are simply going to have to work on your problem together," declared Phoebe. "Now, tell me again what the trouble is?"

"My aqua-lung is too small to allow me to play in the water with my friends. Mom says that I can't submerge and swim under water because I can never hold my breath long enough. It's just a birth defect, but I get teased such an awful lot that I don't like going to the river anymore." The memory of being different made Albert sad again. A tear fell before he could get his emotions under control.

"Have you tried to submerge, Albert?" Phoebe asked.

"No! Mom would kill me if she thought I might try something like that."

"But, how do you know she's right? How do you know for sure you can never swim under water if you never try?"

"But, I'm afraid!" cried Albert.

"That's okay. It's good to be a little scared but you shouldn't let your fear stop you from doing something you really want to do. Come on," said Phoebe, standing up and holding out her hand to Albert, "let's go down to the river right now and try. I'll help you. I promise I won't let anything bad happen to you, okay? Let's go!"

Albert took a deep breath for courage then blew it out. Standing up he said, "All right, I'll try. Just please stay close, okay?"

"You bet! I'll even get into the water with you. It will give me a chance to wash the mud off my shoes and out of my stockings."

So, together they walked, faerie and alligator, through the avocado grove and across a small meadow to the river's edge. Albert took off his tank top, kicked off his shoes and stood looking at the water. Phoebe waited quietly. She knew he was working up his courage to go in and that it was important that he make that decision for himself.

She sat down and took off her muddy shoes and stockings then walked to the river's edge and waded in. She busied herself with her washing trying not to let Albert know she was watching. Then she waded out again to spread her stockings out on the rocks to dry in the sun. She propped her shoes upside down against the same rock to drain.

Albert had watched Phoebe wade in and out of the river with such ease. It seemed so simple. All he had to do was take the first step and wade into the water – 'I'll just get my feet wet,' he thought. And so he did.

Phoebe smiled at Albert standing there in the shallow water. She waded in again and splashed over to where he was standing. The water was a lot deeper for Phoebe than it was for Albert. She was, after all, only eight inches high. But, she could swim, loved to swim, and she did that very well. So, she had no problem treading water next to Albert.

"Why don't you sit down in the water, Albert. It's not very deep for you here. It will help you get used to the idea of being wet. Besides, if you sit down I can stand on your knees and stop treading water. I'm getting tired!" Phoebe really wasn't the least bit tired but she wanted to encourage Albert. So, she had to trick him a little. It worked.

Albert slowly lowered himself into the water and sat on the small river rocks. He was surprised to discover that the water barely came over his tummy. Smiling, he held out a hand to Phoebe and pulled her in to stand on his knee. She looked so cute and much smaller than he first realized. Her tiny wings glistened in the sunlight like a rainbow had been trapped inside. They were so pretty.

Phoebe turned around on his knee and dove off into the water. She splashed around diving under and bobbing back up in another place around Albert, keeping his mind off his fear. Laughing, she scrambled back up on Albert's knee.

"Gosh that's fun," she said. "I just love to swim. Did I tell you I'm on the swim team at school? Everyone says that I swim like a fish. But, for me it's like flying. I feel so light and free in the water. It's fun!"

"You sure looked like you were having a lot of fun. Maybe some day I'll be able to swim like that, too."

"Of course you will! I just know it."

Phoebe splashed around in the water some more and little by little she got Albert to submerge himself a little more. He was having fun splashing around in the water after Phoebe, now. But he hadn't yet pulled together enough courage to put his face in the water. He would soon, she was sure.

Albert must have been reading her mind because he surprised her when he asked, "What do I do now, Phoebe?"

"Well, you need to take a deep breath and then put your face in the water." He gasped at her words so she quickly mentioned that he did not have to put his whole head in the water, just get his nose under.

"Okay," he said. And he took a deep breath then plunged his nose into the water. It felt funny sitting there, head bent with his nose in the water. He realized what he really needed to do to get the right perspective for an alligator was to stretch out completely and lay down in the water first.

He quickly pulled his snout out of the water then carefully lowered himself to a lying position in the water. Taking another deep breath, he submerged his entire head, except for his eyes, under the water. He looked at Phoebe treading water beside him, gave her a quick wink of one eye and then pulled his head all the way down to rest on the river rocks at the bottom.

He felt safe, he realized. He could push himself up out of the water anytime he needed because where he was lying the water was not that deep. He also had Phoebe close by and that gave him courage and a sense of peace within. He was no longer afraid of the water, thanks to her.

They played and swam together for quite a while. Phoebe lead Albert a little further into deeper water each time she circled around him. Albert was holding his breath for more than five minutes at a time when Phoebe reluctantly had to call a stop to their play.

Phoebe happily crawled out of the water and draped herself across one of the big rocks to rest. The rock was warm from the sun and it felt wonderful. She closed her eyes and let the sun dry her clothes.

Albert lay on another rock close by wide-eyed and happy with his experience. He had Phoebe to thank for helping him overcome his fear of the water. He wasn't afraid anymore. Just wait till his friends see him swim! He chuckled to himself.

Phoebe and Albert hugged good-bye at the edge of the avocado grove where they first met. It was time for Phoebe to return home, but she promised Albert that she would come visit him again very soon.

Albert promised that he would keep swimming and holding his breath for longer periods of time. He wanted to prove to everyone that he could submerge just fine in spite of his small aqua-lung. He thanked Phoebe for giving him the courage and the strength to overcome his fear. He was glad to have her for a friend.

"Here," said Phoebe, searching in the pocket of her skirt. "I want you to have this so you can remember me. It's from my favorite spot under a beautiful flowering chestnut tree." She handed Albert the large chestnut.

Albert grinned sheepishly as he accepted the offered gift. He nodded his thanks, afraid that if he said anything he might shed some tears. He didn't want to cry in front of Phoebe.

Phoebe walked back through the underbrush toward the cracked window. The mud had dried out and was hard enough for Phoebe to walk across. She thanked her stars for this small blessing. Halfway across, a slight breeze rustled through her hair and she thought, "I'm going to spread my wings, catch this breeze and fly across this mud to the window." And, with a stretch of her wings she was lifted off her feet.

Pulling the vines away from the window Phoebe was surprised to see that the cracks were a lot smaller. There were also symbols on the screen that were not there before. Somehow, by helping Albert overcome his fear, she had activated the screen, allowing it to come alive once again.

Phoebe studied the new symbols on the screen. She touched an eraser symbol and found that she could wipe the screen clean with her hand. Then she touched an arrow symbol that reminded her of a magic wand. Now, when she touched the screen she created a brand new window, clean and clear with no sign of the cracks it once had. She had fixed the window!

With two taps on the 'Esc' button on her wristwatch, Phoebe was transported back into cyber space two windows. Ram was fast asleep, leaning against the base of the window as she came through. She sat down next to him very quietly. Very slowly she leaned her head over till it rested gently on his shoulder. And waited.

It took Ram a few moments to wake up enough to realize that something was different. He was startled to find Phoebe by his side and he jumped up quickly before he recognized her. Phoebe laughed with such delight that Ram began to laugh as well.

"It's about time you got back, Princess. How did it go?"

"Piece of cake! I even made a new friend. Oh, you can tell Rommy that he was right – those cracked windows do lead into the physical world."

"Wow! Well time to get back and report to Mother Board," said Ram. "She'll be wondering how you managed to get the job done. And, I'm really glad that you came back in one piece!"

"Thanks!" Phoebe beamed at him, full of pride.

With a few more taps on the 'Esc' button, Phoebe was back in the library with Ram. She closed up the file, stacked it with the rest on the table and together she and Ram made their way back to Mother Board's chambers.

She gave her report to Mother Board, explaining everything that had happened to them. Mother Board was very pleased with her work and rewarded Phoebe with a special key. She would explain later how it could be used. But for now it was time for Phoebe to return to her world.

"What assignment do I have for tomorrow?" Phoebe asked.

"Tomorrow is Sunday in your world. It is a day for you to rest and prepare for the next week of school. However, Ram and I will expect to see you next Saturday. Until then, thank you, Phoebe, for the fine work you did for us today. Have a good week."

With a grin on her face, Phoebe gave both Mother Board and Ram a hug. Then she pressed her 'Esc' button one more time, whooshing back to her favorite spot under the flowering chestnut tree. Phoebe looked down at the special key that Mother Board had given her. It was still in her hand! 'Wow!' she thought, 'this cyber key came back with me into the physical world. It really must be special! I wonder what it's for?' She carefully tucked the key into her pocket so it would not get lost. Then Phoebe raced back home, eager to show her parents her new flying skills.

- end-